Stories from Mythology

Stories from Mythology

Swapna Dutta

Illustrations Durga Dutt Pandey

SCHOLASTIC

New York Toronto London Auckland Sydney
Mexico City New Delhi Hong Kong Buenos Aires

For Disha, Nili and Sreya

Published by Scholastic India Pvt. Ltd.
A subsidiary of Scholastic Inc., New York, 10012 (USA).
Publishers since 1920, with international operations in Canada, Australia, New Zealand, the United Kingdom, India, and Hong Kong.

For information regarding permission, write to:
Scholastic India Pvt. Ltd.
A-27, Ground Floor, Sigma Centre
Infocity-1, Sector 34, Gurgaon 122001 (India)

First edition: June 2005
This reprint edition: December 2025

ISBN-13: 978-81-7655-412-1

Printed in India by Saurabh Printers Pvt. Ltd.

Contents

Aruni, an Ideal Student

Long, long ago, there lived a sage named Ayodh Dhaumya. He was a great scholar, and many students from distant lands came to stay in his *gurukul* and learn from him.

Those days there were no schools or colleges. The students lived with the Guru in his ashram, and learnt from him. The well-read *munis* lived a very simple life, and had no servants. The students helped with the housework. They had to get firewood from the forest, fetch water from the river, tend the garden and fields of crops, and also take care of the domestic animals.

They learnt the scriptures, various life skills, how to wield weapons and different arts along with these daily chores. The pupils mastered not just the scriptures but also turned into responsible human beings, ready to face the challenges of life.

One cloudy morning, when the pupils of Ayodh Dhaumya were busy with their usual tasks, it began to rain heavily. Everyone ran indoors. A wild storm blew outside and flashes of lightning streaked across the sky. The thunder roared like hundreds of gunshots being fired here, there, and everywhere. The sage looked worried. He thought of his fields. The crops were nearly ready but Dhaumya had had no time to build strong boundaries. This rain was untimely!

What will happen if the boundaries are washed away by the rain? he wondered. *The entire harvest would be gone.*

He looked at his young pupils and called out to Aruni.

"Aruni, go to the fields and see if the boundaries are still intact. I had noticed some breaks last evening. The water could simply rush in and wash out the crops if the breaks are not mended. Will you attend to it, please?"

"Of course I will, Guruji," said Aruni at once. "I'll mend the boundary and see to it that the water doesn't enter our fields and spoil the crops."

"Do be quick! We need to act fast…" urged Ayodh Dhaumya looking at the grey sky.

Aruni rushed out to the fields. The rain was lashing down in torrents, and most of the fields were already under water. Aruni looked around carefully and noticed the breach in the boundary wall. Water was gushing in from here. With the help of the spade he was carrying, he tried to repair it, blocking the flow with mud and sticks. But the rain in its fury washed it away. The breach only got bigger and bigger. Aruni realised this was a hopeless task.

He was worried and didn't know what to do. And then, he got an idea. The break in the boundary was just about his height. *If I just lie down there instead of*

trying to fix the break, I could stop the water from flowing in, he thought.

Knowing that he didn't have much time, he acted fast. He did not stop to think how cold and clammy the wet earth was! The raindrops felt ice cold on his bare body. But he just lay there quietly, in satisfaction that he was finally able to prevent the water from flowing into the fields. *Now my Guru's crops are safe,* he said to himself. And that was all that mattered to Aruni. He was now the human wall between the water and the fields!

The rains continued through the rest of the day,

without break. Aruni lay there all day, braving the rain. The water pushed against his ribs, trying to enter the fields. He was nearly frozen. But he hardly thought of his own safety.

In the evening, sage Ayodh Dhaumya realised that he had not seen Aruni the whole day.

"Where is Aruni? It's almost night, and I haven't seen him the whole day!" he enquired. "Does anyone know where he is?"

"Guruji, he had gone to check the boundaries of the fields," said one of his disciples. "You asked him to check the water from entering the fields," said another.

"Yes, I did ask him! But that was in the morning. Where has he been all day long? Surely, it wouldn't have taken him so much time to repair the boundary!"

"He never returned from the fields," said the others.

Sage Ayodh Dhaumya looked worried. "I must look for him immediately. I hope he is safe! Come with me, all of you. We must find Aruni at once."

They reached the fields but there was no trace of Aruni anywhere. It was not raining heavily but in the dark night, no one noticed him, lying along the boundary, drenched in mud and water and frozen cold.

"Aruni, are you there?" called the other disciples.

"Aruni! Aruni! Where are you?" called out the sage anxiously.

After moments of silence, a weak voice answered. "I am here, Guruji, lying by the boundary."

"But what are you doing there, son? Why are you lying there in the mud?" asked sage Dhaumya amazed, "Do get up and come here."

"I am afraid, I can't! I have been lying here all day because I could not fix the boundary," said Aruni stuttering with cold. "The rain was too strong. It kept washing away all the mud, the moment I put it there. So I lay down there myself, blocking the water with my body. This was the only thing I could do to save the fields."

Sage Ayodh Dhaumya was touched by his loyalty and obedience.

"Aruni, I am proud of you, my son," he said. He firmly held his shivering body. "Don't worry about the boundary any more. We now have time to repair it as the rain has almost stopped. Come home with me, and let me take care of you." The other students took over fixing of the boundary. Aruni followed his teacher home, happily.

"Aruni, I am really pleased with your sincerity. May you be a great scholar! I give you a new name. From today you shall be known as *Uddalak*, meaning one who rises from the boundary. Everyone will remember you as a shining example of the most obedient and loyal disciple."

Delighted beyond words, Aruni bowed down and touched his Guru's feet.

How Narada Became a Wanderer?

Sage Narada holds an important place in Indian mythology. He is a great scholar of arts and the Veena-playing musician for Gods. A wanderer who roams freely across both heaven and earth, he is often seen as the messenger of Vishnu. The word *nara* means knowledge and *da* is 'one who gives'. So, Narada means a person who passes on knowledge and guides those who seek his advice along the path of right.

Narada, in most of the Purana stories, appears as a scholar but he is also a bundle of playful mischief. He has a naughty, childish streak in him, and he just loves drama! He sometimes discloses the secrets of Gods, demons as well as human beings to those who need not know about these. It sometimes leads to misunderstandings and quarrels between them and this is why Narada is often described as 'one who enjoys quarrels.' Despite his mischievous nature, all Gods, demons and human beings, love him. His ultimate aim is to bring about justice so that the good are rewarded and the bad punished.

Narada is always on the move and never stays in one place for long. This interesting story in the Puranas tells us why he became a wanderer.

Long, long ago there lived a prosperous man named Dakshabrahma. He had many children. He looked forward to the time when they would grow up and help him in his work and finally get married and lead happy lives. But he realised that mere material comfort was not the only source of happiness. He felt spiritual training was also important for the wholesome development of his sons. So he called his sons and spoke to them seriously about how they planned to lead their lives.

"What would you like us to do, father?" asked his sons.

"I'd like you to gain some spiritual knowledge without which no one can truly grow," said Dakshabrahma.

"So, my sons, first go and do penance. Pray to God so that he gives you true knowledge. After that you will return home. That will be the time for you to get married and lead a normal family life."

"Very well, father," agreed the obedient sons. "Where should we go for our *tapasya?*"

"The Himalayas. No one is likely to disturb you there, and you can concentrate on your prayers."

Dakshabrahma's sons left for the Himalayas. They found an appropriate place for meditation along the bank of a crystal clear lake, the *Narayana Saras.* They were soon deep into meditation. This was when Narada happened to pass by and saw them praying. He was curious to know why a group of young boys had left their home and had come up to the Himalayas to pray.

"Who are you?" he asked them.

"We are Dakshabrahma's sons," they replied.

"What are you doing in the Himalayas?" asked Narada.

"Our father asked us to come and pray here," said the eldest. "We shall return home after we have acquired true knowledge."

"And what do you plan to do afterwards?" asked Narada curiously.

"Start our work, get married, of course. And lead the life of a householder," said the boys.

Narada looked them up and down.

Well, here's my chance to have some fun! he thought mischievously.

Turning again to the boys, he said, "Dear boys, what a very foolish thing to do!"

"What do you mean?" they asked in surprise.

"Marriage brings about trouble and problems galore. Why do you wish to be bothered with such things? At the end of your *tapasya*, you will realise the glories of celestial life. And that is the only thing that will give you true happiness.

"I can't think why your father wants you to get trapped into married life. Escape from it while you still have the chance," he went on.

"Think only of the God and aspire for eternity," he emphasised.

"Do you really mean all this?" asked the boys, surprised.

"Of course I do. You are all intelligent, and look at me, have I also not made the choice? I have never allowed thought of marriage to cross my mind, it's sheer waste of energies!" he added.

"Just think about what I have told you, and decide for yourselves!" said Narada. He laughed to himself as he continued with his journey.

Narada's words had a tremendous impact on the minds of Dakshabrahma's sons. They took a solemn vow never to get married. When Dakshabrahma sent for them, they refused to return.

"We have decided to spend the rest of our life in spiritual quest," they informed their father.

Dakshabrahma was greatly upset by their decision. He was looking forward to getting them married and having them and their families with him.

Now he called his younger sons.

"Children, before doing anything else, go and do penance. Pray to God so that he gives you true knowledge. After that you may return home, get married and lead a normal family life. It is your duty to return and help me in my old age and help the family continue," he advised.

The younger sons promised to follow his advice.

Once in the Himalayas for their penance, Narada noticed them and approached the brothers. He repeated the same sermon that he had given to the older brothers. The younger sons felt exactly as their brothers had felt earlier. They also took a vow not to marry and instead take up the path of renunciation. When Dakshabrahma came to know about this, he was very upset indeed. This time he also got to know who had influenced his sons.

Livid with anger, Dakshabrahma faced Narada.

"Why did you mislead my young sons?" he asked Narada.

"I wanted them to marry and settle down, and be near me when I grow old."

"Because I felt it was the right thing to do," Narada replied.

"But it was none of your business! You interfered quite unnecessarily," cried Dakshabrahma.

"Perhaps I did!" admitted Narada.

"I shall not tolerate this. I will curse you," shouted Dakshabrahma.

"Since you did not let my sons settle down, I curse you that you shall never settle down either! Henceforth, you shall be a perpetual wanderer, travelling between heaven and earth. You will not be able to rest in peace in one place."

"Dakshabrahma, it shall be as you wish," said Narada. He did not seem upset really.

Dakshabrahma's curse came to pass and that is why sage Narada turned into a constant wanderer. He is still believed to be wandering somewhere between the heaven and the earth.

Dhruva, the Pole Star

Once upon a time there was a king named Uttanapada. He had two queens, Suniti and Suruchi. Suniti was sweet and good-natured who never hurt anyone in her life. Suruchi, on the other hand, was mean, spiteful and jealous. But of course, she was too clever to show her real self to the king who thought her to be as good as she was beautiful.

Suruchi made Suniti do several things but always kept her in the background. She impressed the king who unfortunately, believed all the untrue tales she made up against Suniti. The king began to love her more than Suniti, and one day things came to such a pass that the king threw Suniti out of the palace. Suniti was expecting his baby but this did not change his decision.

Poor Suniti had no idea why she was being punished like this. But she asked no questions and quietly left the palace. It was difficult for her to walk, as she was feeling unwell. Somehow, she reached the sacred forest where the wise sages lived. The sages knew that Suniti was innocent and that she had been the victim of spiteful Suruchi. They readily gave her shelter, and the wives of the sages looked after her well.

They soon grew fond of her because she was sweet, gentle and helpful. Suniti was also grateful to all of them for whatever they had done for her.

Soon, Suniti had a son, a beautiful, healthy baby who looked like a real prince. He was named Dhruva, or the constant one. Dhruva grew up with the other little boys of the hermitage and shared their chores. He helped gather firewood for the *yajna*s and listened reverently to the sages when they read the scriptures. Everyone at the hermitage loved him.

Growing up amidst pious people, Dhruva soon learned that there was nothing more important than God, who had created the universe. At a tender age, he learned to love God.

The people at the hermitage knew that Dhruva was a prince, and the son of their king, Uttanapada. But no one said anything to Dhruva. One day Dhruva overheard the others talking, and came to know that his father was the king. The five-year old Dhruva ran to his mother.

"Mother, is it true that King Uttanapada is my father?" Dhruva asked Suniti.

"Yes, he is," answered Suniti, wiping her tears.

"But he does not want us – you or me. He threw me out when you were going to be born."

"So you are a queen?" asked Dhruva, his eyes wide open in wonder.

"I was," replied Suniti, "once upon a time. But I have forgotten all about it now."

Little Dhruva made up his mind fast.

"I shall go to see my father," he announced.

"It's no use, my son," said Suniti. "He does not need us. Or else, he would have come to see you long ago." "I don't care. I want to see him. That's all that matters."

"I can't go with you and you are too young to go all that way alone," said Suniti looking worried.

"I am not too young. I want to see my father. I am not afraid to go alone," Dhruva said firmly.

Dhruva left for the palace the very next morning. It took him some time, as his little feet could not carry him too fast. At last he reached the palace. When he entered the gate, the royal guards looked curiously at the little boy.

"Who are you and what do you want?" they enquired.

"I am Dhruva, the son of Queen Suniti," he replied, "I have come to see my father."

The guards recognised him at once. They had noticed his resemblance to the king and let him pass.

"Poor little prince!" said the first guard.

"Hope the king at last gives him his due, all that his stepmother has unfairly snatched from him."

"I wouldn't be too sure," said the second guard shaking his head. "Queen Suruchi is a wicked woman, and has quite bewitched the king."

Dhruva entered the royal hall. The king was seated on the throne.

Queen Suruchi's son Uttam was sitting on his lap.

"Who are you, little boy?" asked the king. In his heart, he already knew the answer because Dhruva looked his mirror image.

"I am Dhruva, your son," said the five-year-old.

He stretched out his arms and said, "Father, I also want to sit on your lap."

Uttanapada's heart melted when he looked at his charming, neglected son. He was about to pick him up in his arms when Suruchi pushed Dhruva away roughly.

"Oh, so you are Suniti's son, are you? Well, you can't sit on his lap. I simply won't allow it."

"But why won't you?" asked Dhruva innocently, "He is *my* father too."

"That may be so. But he disowned your mother. It's only *my* son who has the right to be loved by him. He alone has the right to sit on your father's throne, and be the king when he grows up. You have no place here…"

She continued to say many unkind things that hurt little Dhruva very much.

The king looked on sadly but did not dare protest. He was completely under Suruchi's control, and could not displease her.

Dhruva was in tears. He left the palace but could not forget the unkind words of his stepmother. When he returned home his mother saw his red eyes and trembling lips. She took him in her arms.

"What's wrong, dear? Where have you been? Has anyone been unkind to you?"

"Uttam's mother did not let me talk to father or sit in his lap," Dhruva sobbed.

"What else did she say?" asked Suniti.

"That it was my ill fate to be born as your son and since that was so, I should stop craving for royal things which do not belong to me."

"Perhaps she is right," said Suniti sadly. "Had you been her son, this would never have happened. Nor would you be a stranger to your father."

"Mother, I don't want father's throne or his kingdom or anything that belongs to him. Uttam can have them all," Dhruva continued.

"But I want my father to love me, and give me a little place in his heart. Is there anything I can do about it?"

"Yes you can, my little one," said Suniti. "Pray to Vishnu and tell him about it. That's the best thing that you can do."

"Well, I will," said Dhruva wiping off his tears. "I will go and seek him out myself."

Dhruva set out by himself to seek God the very next morning, just as he had said. He reached the heart of the deep, dark forest and looked around in wonder. He had no idea what Vishnu looked like. As he saw a huge lion approaching him, he ran to it unafraid and put his arms around its neck.

"Are you Vishnu?" he asked the lion. The wild lion moved away quietly without hurting Dhruva. He saw other big and ferocious animals, and asked them the same question. All of them went away from his path without hurting him.

Finally sage Narada, the celestial musician and wanderer, appeared before him.

"Oh, are you Vishnu, then?" asked Dhruva.

"No, I am not," said Narada. "Why do you ask?"

"I have been seeking him all day long, and I don't know what he looks like."

"You are just a little boy! Why do you seek the God at this tender age? Go home and play. You can seek him when you are old enough."

"I don't want to play. I don't want to go back home either, since my own father does not care about me. I only want to find Vishnu and ask for something special from him," said Dhruva in a determined voice.

"Do you think I shall see him?"

"Don't worry, child. You will find him if you call him sincerely from your heart," said sage Narada.

"Will you teach me how? Is it very difficult?" enquired Dhruva.

"Not at all. Just remove all other thoughts from your heart and think of the God alone. Go to *Madhuban*, a sacred forest by the River Kalindi and keep chanting the mantra *Namo Bhagavate Vasudevaya* until he appears before you."

"Thank you. I shall do just as you say," said Dhruva gratefully.

Dhruva left for *Madhuban* at once and did not pause anywhere on the way. He was tired and sleepy but he moved on bravely. When he reached *Madhuban*, he took a dip in the river. He knelt, closed his eyes and repeated the prayer that sage Narada had taught him. He prayed with such concentration and so much sincerity that he totally lost himself in his prayers. He had no sense of heat or cold, day or night, hunger, thirst or sleep. Dhruva had just one thought in his heart – that of Vishnu.

The earnest prayer of the five-year-old boy was so powerful that it sent energy waves all round the universe. The Gods in heaven were afraid that Dhruva might become the King of heaven, when the God appeared before him. The demons were afraid that the purity of his prayers might destroy them totally. Even human kings were afraid that he would become the master of the universe some day. All of them tried their utmost to distract him from his prayers. But they failed miserably.

Vishnu was touched by Dhruva's love and sincerity and appeared before him in all his glory. Suddenly, Dhruva found the whole place full of light and heavy with the fragrance of flowers. Heavenly music played softly. Dhruva opened his eyes to see the wonderful vision of Vishnu standing before him with a smile on his face. His four hands held a conch shell, a *chakra*, a mace and a lotus.

Seeing the Lord in all his glory, Dhruva burst forth in a prayer, which sprang to his lips spontaneously from his heart, known ever since as the *Dhruva Stotra*.

"I am pleased with you little Dhruva," said Vishnu.

"What boon do you want from me? Do you want to be the king?"

"No, my Lord. Let my father give his kingdom to Uttam. But please bless me that I may find a place higher than anyone else, higher than any king. Let that be my permanent place and from there nobody should ask me to go."

"So be it," Vishnu said with a smile.

"You will reign as the king of your land while you are on this earth. But once you die, your place shall be above the sun and the moon. It shall be the highest and most steadfast in the constellation. You shall be the pole star, the most important of them all."

That is how Dhruva became immortal. As the shining pole star, every night he looks down at earth and shows people the right direction.

Proud Garuda

Every God is believed to have his own celestial vehicle. The strong and majestic bird Garuda, carried around Vishnu on his back. He was very proud of this honour because it was he who carried the Lord of the Universe, Vishnu, when he went around conquering the world.

As days went by, Garuda was filled with pride. He terrified the snakes and loved to eat them. They were no match for the great bird so they scuttled into holes and corners whenever they saw him coming. Only one powerful snake – Mani, the son of Ananta Naga, resented this. He hated living this life in constant terror as Garuda, without any warning, would come and grab the first snake he would spot. Mani Naga was smart enough not to get caught but he also realised that he was no match for Garuda. Finally, Mani Naga decided to pray to Shiva for protection and to make Garuda powerless.

Mani Naga prayed for several days. He put his heart and soul into his prayers. At last Shiva appeared before him, pleased by his sincerity and earnestness.

"Well, Mani Naga. I am pleased with you," he said, "What boon would you like to ask of me?"

"Please bless me that I may always have your protection. Garuda should not be able to harm me in any way. I am tired of living in constant fear," said Mani Naga.

"Very well, it shall be just as you wish. From this moment, you need not fear Garuda any more," pronounced Shiva.

Mani Naga heaved a sigh of relief. He was also jubilant as he could now teach Garuda a lesson. He went straight to Vishnu's abode, where Garuda lived. Mani Naga moved around defiantly, choosing the most prominent places so that Garuda might see him.

Garuda saw him but could not bear this sight. *A mere snake defying me, the mighty Garuda!* he thought.

"What do you mean by parading in front of me like this, Mani Naga?" cried Garuda angrily. "Aren't you afraid of me?"

"Afraid of you? Of course not," said Mani Naga, tossing his hood.

"You must be out of your senses! Don't you know that I can gobble you up this instant, in one single mouthful?"

"Just try it and see," hissed Mani Naga.

Garuda had just finished a huge meal and his stomach was full. He did not feel like eating just then. *I cannot allow this creature to be cheeky!* he thought.

Garuda grabbed Mani Naga by his tail, and locked him up in his room.

"I'll have you for my dinner tonight," said Garuda. "That should teach you a lesson!" Poor Mani Naga was terrified, and did not know what to do.

He did not expect this after being blessed by Shiva.

In the meantime, Nandi, Shiva's *vahana*, noticed that Mani Naga had not returned home that evening. He went straight to Shiva.

"My Lord," he said, "I am sure Mani Naga is in some danger. He has not returned home. Perhaps Garuda has eaten him up, after all."

Shiva closed his eyes for a moment, and saw what had happened. He blamed himself for having forgotten his promise to Mani Naga.

"Well, my Lord? What did you see?" asked Nandi.

"Mani Naga is not dead, Nandi, but I am afraid Garuda has locked him up in his room."

"What do we do now, my Lord?" asked Nandi, "You know, you had promised to protect him."

"Go to Vishnu immediately, and pray to him. When he offers you a boon, ask him for Mani Naga, and bring him along with you," said Shiva.

Nandi dashed off to Vishnu's abode and knelt before him in earnest prayer. Vishnu was pleased and Nandi asked him for Mani Naga.

"Very well," said Vishnu, "I shall ask Garuda to release Mani Naga immediately. You can take him back to Kailasa with you."

Nandi bowed his head and expressed his gratitude for granting his prayer.

Garuda was getting ready to eat his dinner when Vishnu sent for him. "Why have you sent for me at this hour, my Lord?" he asked in an insolent voice.

"Garuda, I want you to release Mani Naga at once and let him go with Nandi," said Vishnu.

"Certainly not!" said Garuda. "You know how I enjoy eating snakes. I have captured him and he belongs to me rightfully."

"Even then, I am asking you to let him go," said Vishnu.

"I shall NOT let him off," said Garuda in an arrogant tone.

"My Lord, it is not fair that you should ask me to give up what belongs to me."

Vishnu was astonished at Garuda's arrogance. Nandi was also shocked.

"Do you know what you are saying, Garuda? I think you are forgetting yourself," Vishnu said sternly.

"I am not forgetting myself at all," said Garuda, tossing his head. "It's *you*, forgetting what you owe me. It is because I carry you everywhere on my back that you are able to go where you please. You are victorious in every battle on my account. You were able to conquer the demons because of *me*."

Vishnu should have been very angry with Garuda's absurd boasting. But instead, he burst out laughing.

"I don't see why you should laugh at my words," said Garuda arrogantly. "What I said is absolutely true."

"Oh well," said Vishnu still laughing, "so I am victorious because of you, is it? And I am able to move around because of you?"

"Of course..." said Garuda.

"Garuda!" cried Nandi, horrified, "What are you saying? How can you even think such a thing? Your pride will destroy you totally if you go on like this. Beg for Vishnu's pardon at once."

"Leave Garuda alone, Nandi," Vishnu said in a gentle voice. "I shall deal with him."

He turned to Garuda. "Well, Garuda," he said giving him a searching look, "I do admit that you are very strong. Only a very strong person can possibly carry me. Now, tell me, can you bear the weight of my small toe? Just my small toe and nothing else?"

"I don't understand what you mean by that, my Lord," said Garuda amazed, "I carry the whole of you on my back, don't I?"

"Very well. Let me rest just my small toe on your back," said Vishnu and placed his small toe on Garuda's back. Its weight squashed Garuda's neck flat in an instant and went right inside Garuda's shoulder. In a moment Garuda was nothing but a twisted lump of feathers.

"I am sorry, my Lord," cried Garuda in panic, "Please have mercy on me. I now see how very absurd my pride was. You are the Lord and master. The only power I have is what *you* choose to bless me with. I realise that now."

"Are you quite sure you do?" asked Vishnu.

"Yes, my Lord," cried Garuda in a humble voice. "I made a grave mistake because my pride made me blind. I can see it all and I am sorry. Do please forgive me."

Just then Goddess Lakshmi appeared, disturbed by the noise. She felt very sorry to see Garuda's crumpled body.

"Please forgive Garuda, my Lord," she pleaded. "I am sure he has paid the price of his pride. He must be in great pain. Please give him back his original form. He looks so terrible with his body all twisted up."

"Not as yet," said Vishnu firmly. "Pride and ingratitude are two vices. Garuda must learn that this could lead to his ruin. Nandi, take Garuda and Mani Naga to Shiva. Garuda will get back his original form only if he succeeds in pleasing Shiva with his prayers."

Nandi took both of them to Kailasa and narrated the incident to Shiva.

Garuda began praying to Shiva and begged for his mercy. Shiva finally felt sorry for him and said, "Go and take a dip in the Gautami Ganga. You will get back your original body. But do not ever forget what happens to people who are proud and ungrateful."

Garuda thanked Shiva and rushed to the celestial river. He jumped into the water and when he rose, he felt as strong, powerful and handsome as ever. Garuda really learnt his lesson. From then on, he never allowed pride to go to his head ever again!

Theft of the Parijat Tree

Indra, the King of heaven, had *Nandan Kanan*, the most wonderful garden you can imagine! It had all the beautiful and sweet-scented flowers that grow on earth and many more that were out of the world. The pride of the garden was the parijat, a tree that bore delicate white flowers with the most exquisite fragrance. Its aroma filled up the entire place. Parijat was the favourite of Indrani, the wife of Indra. She loved to wear the flowers in her hair and waited for everyone to tell her how the flowers added to her charm. Indrani never shared the flowers with anyone else and came to regard the parijat as her special property.

One bright morning, Krishna and his wife Satyabhama decided to visit Indra. He received them personally and took them to his palace. After some rest, Indra requested them to take a walk in his famous garden. The flowers that bloomed in all the colours of the rainbow delighted Satyabhama.

She walked among them, admiring one flower after another. Finally her eyes fell on the parijat.

"What is this wonderful flower?" she asked Krishna.

"It is the parijat," replied Krishna.

"I haven't seen this flower before," remarked Satyabhama. "Where did Indra get it from?"

"The parijat came up along with many other things when the great ocean was churned by the gods and the demons to obtain the elixir of life. That's when Indra took it, and brought it to his garden," replied Krishna.

For a moment, Satyabhama was lost in thought. She looked up and said, "But this was not right of Indra. If the parijat came up at the time of the churning of the ocean then it is common property and should belong to everyone, not just one person. In any case, I fail to see why it should belong to Indra alone. He hasn't done anything special to deserve it. Has he?"

"Perhaps you are right," agreed Krishna, "the parijat ought to be enjoyed by all. You rightly said it is not Indra's personal property."

"Then let us take it away to the earth," said Satyabhama eagerly. "I shall plant it in my garden and share the flowers with everyone in Dwarka."

"Very well, if that's what you wish," said Krishna.

"Yes, I do desire it," said Satyabhama. "I shall wear the flowers in my hair and if people outside Dwarka ask for them, they too shall have them."

Krishna smiled and pulled up the parijat tree from its roots. He laid it on the back of Garuda, who was waiting to carry them back to the earth.

Just as they were about to start, the guards at the

gate of *Nandan Kanan* stopped them.

"Stop!" they cried. "Where are you taking the parijat? It belongs to our queen, Indrani. You cannot steal it."

"Stealing?" cried Satyabhama, "This tree came up at the time of churning of the ocean and is not anyone's personal property. We have every right to take it back to earth and let everyone enjoy its flowers. It is selfish to keep it to yourself."

"You cannot steal the parijat. Indra will fight you and you cannot stand up to him," said the guards contemptuously. "All the Gods will back him up as well. What can a single person like you do against our heavenly force? Better give up the tree and get back to earth before anyone realises what you were about to do."

"How dare you!" cried Satyabhama, her eyes flashing. "Go and tell Indra that we are taking away the parijat. Let him fight Krishna if he dares."

The guards rushed to inform Indra about the invasion. They also repeated Satyabhama's words to Indrani who was livid with rage. "How dare Satyabhama, a mere human being, criticise the queen of heaven and steal her property? Indra, you must teach them a lesson!" she shouted.

"Krishna may be an incarnation of Vishnu, but at the moment he is the prince of Dwarka and belongs to the human race. He cannot annoy the inmates of heaven," Indrani continued.

Indra picked up the lightning, his chief weapon, and prepared to fight Krishna. All the Gods and stars in heaven supported him. Getting back the parijat was now a matter of prestige and they could not possibly allow Krishna to take it away.

Indra, accompanied by his entire army faced Krishna, who stood alone with just Garuda by his side. Crores of angels along with Indra shot their arrows towards Krishna. They covered the entire sky shutting out the light completely. But Krishna destroyed all their weapons with great ease! Varuna arrived with his own special missile but Garuda instantly broke it to pieces. Yama, the King of death threw his mace at Krishna. But this broke into pieces, the moment it touched Krishna's mace. Kubera dashed in to attack Krishna, only to see his chariot going to pieces.

The sun and the moon came out with their fury but a mere glance of Krishna cooled their fire and completely put out their light. Agni, the God of fire also froze at a glance from Krishna. Finally, no one from the celestial army survived except Indra himself. Alone, he was now face to face with Krishna. Indra held his main weapon, the lightning, while Krishna took up his *Sudarshan Chakra.* Indra's lightning was said to be invincible and he shuddered with fear as he threw it at Krishna. But Krishna grabbed it by his free hand and the lightning turned to a handful of frost. Now Indra was completely weaponless. There was no need for Krishna to fight him. Defeated and defenceless, Indra tried to run away, burning in shame and humiliation. Who could have imagined that a mere prince from the earth could defeat the King of heaven and his entire army?

Satyabhama burst out laughing as she saw Indra running away. "Well, is that the King of heaven, running away?" she asked him. "Don't worry, I am not going to take away your precious parijat. You can take it back to Indrani. I was a guest in your house but Indrani is so proud that she didn't even bother to come and greet me. Is that the way the God of Gods treats his guests? That's why I was angry and wanted to let her know that pride has its fall. I have no wish to take anything which she thinks is hers."

Indra came back and sought Satyabhama's pardon. "It was very wrong of my wife to ignore a guest of honour. Please forgive us both and take the parijat with you. And please don't be angry with us any more."

"Are you saying this because Krishna defeated you?" asked Satyabhama.

"No. I am not ashamed to be defeated by Krishna, the incarnation of Vishnu himself. I would really like you to have the parijat."

"But it belongs to your *Nandan Kanan,*" said Krishna. "I had picked it up at the request of Satyabhama because I too felt that the Queen of heaven should be shown how to respect guests. I think I have succeeded, so please say no more. The parijat shall remain where it has been all this time. Here it is."

"Please Krishna, take it to Dwarka now," begged Indra. "When your days on earth are over, the original tree can return to heaven once more."

"So be it," said Krishna with a smile.

Krishna and Satyabhama soon sat on Garuda, holding the parijat carefully. They were off to Dwarka with their prized possession.

Usha's Dream

Many years ago, Vana, the King of demons, pleased Shiva with his devotion. For his great *tapasya*, he won a boon that he would remain invincible to all, both on the heaven and the earth.

Vana had a beautiful daughter named Usha. Her great friend and constant companion was Chitralekha, the daughter of one of Vana's ministers. As Usha grew up, she began to wonder who her husband would be. She did not like any of the demon princes or her father's young friends.

It was a strange night! It changed Usha's life forever. She dreamt of a handsome prince who sat beside her and smiled at her, looking deep into her eyes. Usha fell in love with him instantly and woke up to find that it was only a dream. But something deep within her told her that this dream meant something significant and that such a prince must exist somewhere.

Usha was no longer her old self. Her love for the dream prince was so real that she could think of nothing and no one else. She went around lost in her own thoughts, longing for him and missing him with all her heart. Her friends teased her, especially when they realised that she had no idea who he was and had merely seen him in her dream.

"Come on, Usha, wake up!" said her friends. "You can't take a dream that seriously."

"I can't help it. I can think of nothing else," said Usha looking miserable. "I know he must exist somewhere. I also know that I cannot live without him, whoever he is."

"But that's the whole point! You don't even know who he is. You don't know if he is real, what his name is and where he lives," said her friends. "How on earth will you ever find him? Where will you begin? You know absolutely nothing!"

"I know all that. Nevertheless, I have to find him. I have already accepted him in my heart as my husband, and shall wed no other man," said Usha.

The others laughed and thought she had gone crazy. But Chitralekha realised how serious Usha was and decided to make an attempt to find out if such a person really existed.

Chitralekha was a very talented artist, and could draw anyone's portrait very accurately.

"If I were to draw portraits of all the young kings and princes, would you recognise your dream prince, if he happens to be one of them?" asked Chitralekha.

"Of course," said Usha without any hesitation.

"I remember him so clearly. But can you really draw portraits of all the princes? There must be so many of them!"

"I must try," said Chitralekha. "It's the only way to find out if he is real or just a dream."

"Please hurry then, I pray to you. Please...," said Usha, "I shall be eternally grateful to you if you can find him for me."

Chitralekha got busy from the next day, drawing portraits of prince after prince. At night she would take all the portraits and show them to Usha. The princess looked at them eagerly but turned down all of them with a heavy heart. Chitralekha got to work again, drawing and showing them to Usha. One night, Usha picked up the first portrait listlessly. She sat up eagerly and looked at it again. "Who is this?" she asked Chitralekha.

"It is not my prince but he reminds me of someone."

"It is Krishna, the prince of Dwarka," said Chitralekha, "People say that he is an incarnation of Vishnu."

"Show me the next one," said Usha. Chitralekha handed it to her.

Usha frowned, trying to recall something.

"Strange! This person reminds me of someone too. Who is he?"

"It is Pradyumna, Krishna's son."

"It is not my prince, though he does remind me of him. I wonder why," said Usha.

"How about this one?" asked Chitralekha handing her another portrait.

Usha looked at the portrait and stood still as a statue.

"Well?" asked Chitralekha looking at her curiously.

"Who .... is .... he?" whispered Usha hardly able to speak.

"It is Aniruddha, Pradyumna's son. He is the grandson of Krishna," said Chitralekha.

"He is the prince of my dreams," cried Usha.

"Are you quite sure?" asked Chitralekha.

"As sure as I am alive. I remember this smiling face, these eyes that stared at me and the hands that held mine. Chitralekha, he is the one I have been waiting for, all my life," said Usha in excitement.

"Now that we know that he really exists, I shall die if I cannot marry him. Please, I beg of you, bring him to me."

Chitralekha was deep in thought as she walked up and down.

She knew it was impossible for her to meet Aniruddha, let alone bring him to the palace. Aniruddha lived with his father and grandfather at Dwarka, surrounded by hills and deep moats. She had heard that anyone wishing to go there secretly had to scale seven steep walls and conquer a regular army of guards. Moreover, the invincible C*hakra* of Krishna was always revolving across the skies of Dwarka, ready to destroy the strangers.

"I am absolutely certain that anyone coming from the land of demons, would not be admitted to the hallowed kingdom of Dwarka," Chitralekha told Usha. But the princess was not convinced.

"I don't care how tough it is. If you love me and are my true friend, bring Aniruddha here to me."

"I shall try. But I don't have much hope of success. I fail to see how I can ever get inside the city walls of Dwarka," remarked Chitralekha.

But true to her promise, Chitralekha started on her hazardous journey keeping her friend's happiness in mind. She was just wondering how to proceed when she caught sight of the wandering sage Narada, singing the glories of Vishnu.

Chitralekha rushed to him with folded hands. Narada blessed her and asked where she was going alone. She narrated the whole story and begged for his help.

Narada smiled.

"So be it. I shall grant you a special power that will enable you to reach not just Dwarka but the place where Aniruddha is at the moment," Narada said.

"You will be able to tell him about your friend Usha and also take him back to your own kingdom with you."

Chitralekha was overjoyed. She touched his feet again, this time in heartfelt gratitude.

Narada went away playing on his veena. A naughty smile was on his lips. Narada had a mischievous streak in him and he enjoyed watching people get into a fight. He knew that this would lead to a fight between the

Yadavas and the demons. But he was happy as this was going to amuse him no end!

Chitralekha soon found herself within the gates of Dwarka, just as Narada had said. To her surprise, no one made any attempt to stop her. People were actually directing her to the palace where prince Aniruddha was. It was evening, and the grand hall was gorgeously decorated. A group of musicians played exquisite music while a beautiful dancer performed at the centre.

But prince Aniruddha sat listlessly in the front, watching the performance. He looked morose, and his thoughts seemed to be wandering. Chitralekha walked up to him and whispered who she was and from where she had come. She also told him about Usha's strange dream.

Aniruddha's face lit up.

"Is she real, then? The beautiful princess of my dreams? I also saw a similar dream and since then, I have not been able to think of anything else."

"She is just as real as you are," said Chitralekha laughing, "And what's more, she says she will marry no one but you. That is why I have come to take you to her."

"Can you really take me to Usha? I have no idea where your kingdom lies," said Aniruddha looking worried.

"We need not worry about that," said Chitralekha. "Thanks to sage Narada's blessings, we shall reach there as soon as you are ready to leave."

"Let's go," said Aniruddha eagerly. "I can't wait to see her again."

Chitralekha closed her eyes, prayed and once again sought sage Narada's help. True to his promise, they soon found themselves inside Usha's palace.

In the meantime, Usha had been feeling both sad and worried. She had no hope of Chitralekha actually reaching Dwarka or of finding her prince. She blamed herself bitterly for having made her go and feared that she might be in danger now. She could not believe her eyes when she saw Chitralekha walking into her room with prince Aniruddha.

"At last!" said Aniruddha smiling at her.

"At last!" said Usha looking into his eyes.

"Go and fetch the garlands. Blow the conch-shell," said Chitralekha to her other friends. "We must arrange the wedding of Usha and Aniruddha since her father might not give his consent to the marriage."

Everyone rushed around getting things ready quietly. Usha and Aniruddha exchanged garlands and went through a *gandharva* wedding, needing no priest.

But Usha and Aniruddha's happiness was short-lived. The news of a stranger in the palace of princess Usha, soon reached King Vana. He was mad with rage and ordered his soldiers to capture him at once. But Aniruddha was a brave fighter, like his father Pradyumna and grandfather Krishna. Aniruddha soon defeated the army single-handed. The soldiers of Vana fell like ninepins and soon he had no opposition.

When Vana heard the news, he appeared himself on the battlefield.

But Aniruddha fought him bravely and wounded him severely. Vana soon realised that there was no way he could defeat Aniruddha, at least not in a straight and open warfare. So he resorted to a trick and got snakes to bind up his hands, feet and his entire body so that Aniruddha could not move at all.

In the meantime, Narada went to Dwarka and informed the Yadavas about the fate of Aniruddha. Both Krishna and Pradyumna had been worried at the sudden disappearance of Aniruddha. They immediately set forth and reached the kingdom of Vana. Soon a great battle raged between the two sides. Shiva, who had granted Vana his power, came to assist him along with Kartikeya. The fight was now between Shiva and Krishna, the incarnation of Vishnu.

Krishna set off a magic missile that made Shiva yawn so much that he was hardly able to hold his weapon in his hand. And Garuda bit Kartikeya so badly that he too was unable to wield his weapon and was forced to leave the battlefield. Balarama, Krishna's elder brother, pitched in with his plough, setting armies of demons slumping down in pain. Meanwhile, Aniruddha's father, Pradyumna fought steadily at another end.

When Vana saw that there was hardly any soldier left to fight for him, he came to fight Krishna himself, holding all his powerful weapons in his hundred hands.

He tried the most lethal weapons in his collection, and the fight soon took on an alarming dimension. Finally, Krishna let off his invincible *Sudarshan Chakra*. It could not kill Vana as Shiva himself had granted him life, but the *Chakra* cut off Vana's hundred arms.

Seeing Vana stripped off all his power, Shiva walked up to Krishna and held his hands.

"Krishna, do forgive Vana. After all, it was I who had granted him the boon that he could conquer

everyone on earth. That is why he got so wild and unruly. But I think he has now learned his lesson. Please forgive him for my sake."

Krishna smiled and said, "Very well, it shall be as you wish. Since Vana has been enjoying your blessings and protection all this while, he shall enjoy mine as well."

As Krishna walked up to the place where Aniruddha lay strangled by snakes, Garuda followed him there. The snakes left Aniruddha and fled in fear at the sight of Garuda. Aniruddha sat up and opened his eyes. He was amazed to see his grandfather and father, who hugged him affectionately.

Vana came to them soon after and begged Krishna's pardon and Pradyumna's too. In a moment, all hatred was forgotten and all bitterness, swept aside. Everyone merrily joined in the celebrations when Usha and Aniruddha were married once again with great pomp and splendour. After that, the entire party along with the newly-wed bride and groom left for Dwarka, where a great welcome awaited them.

How the Tulasi Became a Sacred Tree?

One day Indra, the King of heaven, went to Kailasa to visit Shiva. He noticed a fierce-looking man guarding the door but there was no one else in sight. Indra enquired about Shiva but the man simply looked through him and did not answer.

"Please tell me where Shiva is..." asked Indra, "I have come specially to see him."

Indra asked him again and again and when he received no answer, he got so angry that he threw his weapon of lightning at him. But strangely, the lightning did not even touch the man. On the contrary, a whiff of flame burst from his brow and was about to engulf Indra, who instantly realised that the fierce looking man was none other than Shiva himself. Indra went down on his knees and begged Shiva's pardon. Since it was a genuine mistake and Indra had no intention of insulting Shiva, the latter forgave Indra readily. Shiva then grasped the seething flame from his brow and threw it into the ocean.

As the flame fell into the swirling water, a strange thing happened. The flame instantly turned into a little child and started crying. The ocean took him in her arms and rocked him quiet. Brahma, who had also

arrived at Kailasa just then, saw the little boy in the arms of the ocean.

"Who is he? What is his name?" Brahma asked the ocean.

"Why don't you give him a name, my Lord?" asked the ocean.

Brahma picked up the child in his arms. He named the child Jalandhara and blessed him with a number of boons. The most important one was that no one on earth would be able to vanquish Jalandhara except Shiva himself. Brahma then made him the King of demons.

Jalandhara grew up to be a powerful young man. Because of his special boon from Brahma, no one was able to control him in any way. He won every battle with ease and soon came to be known as the invincible Jalandhara. He lived happily with wife Vrinda, the beautiful daughter of Kalnemi, a powerful *asura.*

But Jalandhara had fought and conquered nearly everyone except the mighty Indra. With Brahma's blessings as his armour, Jalandhara fought the Gods and captured Indra's kingdom. Indra, driven out by the mighty Jalandhara, sought Shiva's help.

"My Lord, I shall be totally undone if you do not save me from Jalandhara," he pleaded. "It is not enough to save me. Jalandhara must be killed or he will strike again and yet again, and none of us will have a moment of peace."

"Do not worry, Indra," assured Shiva, "I shall

vanquish Jalandhara. He will not be able to withstand me as he was born of the flame from my brow."

Shiva came out of Kailasa to fight Jalandhara and a terrible battle followed. Vrinda, who was an ardent devotee of Vishnu, prayed to him earnestly, and begged him to protect Jalandhara from Shiva. Vishnu could not refuse so earnest a prayer and kept saving Jalandhara from every blow. Shiva soon found that he was unable to overpower Jalandhara as he was under Vishnu's protection. Things came to a total standstill. The Gods now started praying to Vishnu so that he would withdraw his protection. Otherwise it was quite impossible to harm Jalandhara.

Vishnu realised that something must be done about Jalandhara since he could not allow him to displace Indra and the Gods from heaven. And yet he could do nothing as long as Vrinda continued praying to him. In the meantime, Jalandhara confronted Shiva and said, "I have already conquered heaven and earth and have driven Indra and his Gods away. And now I will conquer you!"

"Don't even try it," said Shiva smiling at him. "You will be inviting destruction on yourself!"

"You don't know who you are talking to," said Jalandhara in an arrogant voice. "I am invincible. Don't you know that I have driven out Indra, the King of heaven? I'm not afraid of you."

"Indeed!" said Shiva and he placed one foot in the ocean. He drew a *chakra* on the waves with his right toe. This flashed like lightning and rotated on the water at great speed. “Pick up the *chakra*, Jalandhara,” said Shiva. “I shall fight with you only if you are able to lift it from the water.”

“Ha! That’s no big deal!” said Jalandhara bending down to pick up the *chakra*.

Meanwhile, unknown to Jalandhara, something else had happened.

Vishnu, knowing that Jalandhara would remain invincible so long as Vrinda continued her prayer, appeared before Vrinda. He was in the guise of Jalandhara. Vrinda was deceived. She stopped praying to Vishnu and stood up to greet her husband. This was the moment when Jalandhara remained unprotected. Being extremely strong, he was able to lift Shiva’s *chakra* from the water but as he did not possess Vishnu’s protection, the *chakra* cut his body into two.

Jalandhara died because Vishnu had tricked Vrinda. She was extremely angry and was about to curse Vishnu when he appeared before her. “How could you do this to me, my Lord?” she cried reproachfully. “Why did you play this trick on me?”

“I had no other option, my child,” said Vishnu, “just think of my dilemma. I could not let down a devotee who prayed as earnestly as you did. So your husband, for whose safety you prayed, remained unharmed. At the same time, I could not let down Indra or the Gods, who also prayed to me to protect them from your husband. Besides, I could not allow

Jalandhara to create such havoc on heaven and earth. So I had to interrupt your prayer somehow. And this was the only way."

"You cheated me," said Vrinda again.

"No mortal lives forever," said Vishnu. "Jalandhara has lived his life. And because Shiva himself vanquished him, Jalandhara will enjoy a special place in heaven. Do not grieve for him, Vrinda. It's the best thing that could have happened to him."

Vishnu sought her forgiveness and said, "Vrinda, you are one of my best and truest devotees. I bless you that henceforth you will remain an integral part of my worship. Anyone who worships me, will remember you too." When Vrinda died and was cremated, a beautiful and aromatic tree sprang up from her ashes. This was the Tulasi tree!

Since then, the leaves of Tulasi are considered essential for the worship of Vishnu.

Prahlada's Devotion

Once upon a time there lived a king named Hiranyakasipu. He was the King of demons. He wanted to be supremely powerful so he prayed to Brahma and received a boon from him that no God, man or beast would ever be able to kill him. Once he got the boon, he became so very arrogant that he decided that there was no need for a God Almighty. He told all his people that he was their Chief, and that they should worship him alone. He ordered all temples to be destroyed and made it clear that so long as he was around, there was no place for any other God. If anyone dared worship Vishnu, Shiva or anyone other than himself, his only punishment would be death. In fact, Hiranyakasipu thought that Vishnu was his greatest enemy.

Hiranyakasipu had a small son named Prahlada. He was sent to the *gurukul* to be educated as befitted a prince. On his return, Hiranyakasipu asked him, "Well, my son, tell me briefly what you have learned from your teachers at the *gurukul.*"

"Dear father, I can sum up all my learning in a few words. I worship Vishnu, who has no beginning, and no end; who is the cause of all things; whom no power on earth can destroy."

Hiranyakasipu was so angry to hear these words that he trembled with rage. His anger was first directed towards Prahlada's teachers.

"You traitors! Did I entrust my little son to your care so that you might teach him to love and revere my bitter enemy? I shall have you put to death."

"It is not our fault, great king," cried the teachers, "We did not tell Prahlada a word of what he has just said. Nor did we teach him anything about your sworn enemy."

"Tell me, Prahlada, who has told you all this?" asked Hiranyakasipu.

"Why father, it is the Lord himself who has taught me this because he resides in everything we see around us. He dwells in mountains and trees, the sky and the oceans. He dwells in the innermost heart of every man," replied Prahlada.

"He is the Supreme, the God of Gods, and the King of kings," he continued.

"Don't you dare speak like this!" screamed Hiranyakasipu. "Don't you know that I am the only King of the three worlds? There is no other God."

"The Lord is in you as well, my father," said Prahlada. "All of us, everything on earth, are a part of God."

"Don't you dare call anyone else 'the supreme being' while I am around," yelled Hiranyakasipu. "You fool, don't force me to put you to death. That is the only punishment I have for those who worship anyone except me."

"But father, the Lord is the creator, protector and destroyer of the universe," said Prahlada, "Why are you so unwilling to acknowledge this simple truth? It is at his wish that we live or die."

Hiranyakasipu mopped his brow in rage. "Take this fool away, out of my sight. I shall give one more chance to his teachers. Let them teach him what the actual truth is."

So Prahlada was sent to the *gurukul* once again with strict instructions to teach him about the glories and omnipotence of Hiranyakasipu and keep off all thoughts of Vishnu. But when Prahlada returned the second time, he once again sang praises of Vishnu and his all-pervasiveness. This time Hiranyakasipu was angry beyond words.

"This boy is a disgrace to our clan! I gave him several chances because he is so young. But he is simply no good. Take him away and kill him. That's the only thing to do," he told his soldiers. Then he looked at his son and said, "I hope you realise your mistake in not obeying me when you die. Tell me, are you not afraid?"

"No, father," said Prahlada smiling fearlessly, "I am not afraid so long as I have Vishnu as my protector. I know that no weapon can hurt me."

"Indeed!" cried Hiranyakasipu, livid with rage, as he struck Prahlada with the sword in his hand. But Prahlada felt no pain. The sword turned as soft as a flower as it touched Prahlada's body. It did not even leave a single scratch!

Hiranyakasipu ordered his men to throw Prahlada before a mad elephant that had crushed several people to death. But the elephant stopped in front of Prahlada, picked him up gently and put him on his back.

"Lock him up in the dungeon with the most poisonous snakes," ordered Hiranyakasipu. But none of the snakes harmed Prahlada and their venom turned to nectar in Prahlada's presence.

"What magic have you been using against these creatures?" Hiranyakasipu roared.

"I know no magic, father," replied Prahlada, "The snakes did not harm me because they too are a part of the Lord and knew that I had the Lord's protection. Father, God is everywhere and in everything, living and non-living. That is why I am not afraid. Do try to believe and understand this."

Hiranyakasipu thought hard about other ways of killing him. His pride had completely blinded him to his love for his son. He had started looking at him as his enemy. "Throw Prahlada from the top of the highest tower," he ordered. "He will surely die when he falls from that height."

But the moment Prahlada was pushed from the tower, the earth below grew as soft as a bed and Prahlada was not hurt at all.

"Throw him into the deep ocean. Tie heavy stones on his body so that he might sink to the bottom,"

Hiranyakasipu thundered. Prahlada uttered Vishnu's name as he fell into the ocean, and the stones turned to sand and melted into the sea while the waves kept Prahlada afloat until a big wave gently dropped him on the shore. Then he walked back to the palace unhurt.

Hiranyakasipu could not believe his eyes when he saw his son. He thought his men had not carried out their duty.

"I shall have to destroy him with my own hands," he told himself. He ordered a huge fire to be lit. He caught hold of Prahlada and threw him into the middle of the flames. Once again, as Prahlada prayed to Vishnu, the flames all round him turned cold and he remained unhurt.

When Hiranyakasipu realised that Prahlada could not be destroyed either by him or by any of his men, he got desperate.

"Tell me, Prahlada, do you really believe that God exists in everything?"

"Indeed I do, father," replied Prahlada. "If you shared my belief, you would not be so unhappy today."

"I don't believe it," said Hiranyakasipu. "Does God also exist in this pillar?" he asked pointing to a thick pillar behind him.

"Yes," Prahlada said with conviction.

"I don't believe you," said Hiranyakasipu, kicking the pillar. The pillar collapsed into a heap of rubble and Vishnu stepped out of the pillar in the form of Narsimha, half-man and half-lion. Hiranyakasipu tried

to fight him but was vanquished by him.

Hiranyakasipu had enjoyed the boon that no man or animal could destroy him. But Vishnu, appearing as Narsimha, half-man and half-lion, destroyed him easily. Prahlada was aware that Narsimha was none other than Vishnu himself. He knelt down before him and prayed, "My Lord, forgive my father."

"Don't grieve for your father, my child," said Narsimha, "He has lost his arrogance and pride and will now attain a special place in my abode. Tell me, what boon should I grant you?"

"Now that I have seen you with my eyes, I have nothing left to wish for, my Lord," said Prahlada. "Just let me remain your ardent devotee forever."

"So you shall, my child," said Narsimha, "but your work on earth is not yet complete. You have to live your life first."

Narsimha made Prahlada the King of the demons and he lived to be one of the best kings on earth.

Harishchandra and Taramati

Long, long ago there lived a king in Ayodhya named Harishchandra. He was the most generous king on the earth. His reputation as an unconditional 'giver' spread far and wide. When sage Vishwamitra, who was known for his temper, heard this, he decided to visit King Harishchandra himself and check out his reputation.

Sage Vishwamitra held a grievance against King Harishchandra. A short while ago, five heavenly nymphs from Indra's court had secretly entered his hermitage and stolen all the flowers. Vishwamitra was very annoyed with them. He ordered the creepers in the garden to entwine themselves around the *apsaras* and take them prisoner. When the *apsaras* cried out for help, King Harishchandra, who was passing by, had set them free. Ever since that incident, Vishwamitra was very angry with Harishchandra. Now he wanted to see if Harishchandra was prepared to make amends.

As soon as King Harishchandra saw sage Vishwamitra enter his palace, he came down from his throne and welcomed him. He showed his respect by washing his feet and making sure that Vishwamitra was comfortable.

"Well Harishchandra," said Vishwamitra without

any preamble, "I am told you are the most generous king on earth. Tell me, what are you prepared to give a sage like me?"

"Anything you desire, my Lord," replied Harishchandra readily. "It is yours for the asking."

"Indeed!" said Vishwamitra with a sneer, "Easy enough to say it! But are you really prepared to do it?"

"Try me and see," said Harishchandra modestly with a smile, "I feel honoured to be of service to you."

"Not refusing small favours is not a difficult thing to do, especially if one is a king," said Vishwamitra. "But what if I were to ask for something really big?"

"Please let me know what your wish is. I will be very happy to carry it out for you," said Harishchandra, wondering what Vishwamitra had in mind and why he had such a mysterious smile.

"Very well. I trust you," said Vishwamitra, "But later, don't say that I didn't caution you."

All the people present looked curiously at sage Vishwamitra and he stared at them. "All of you here and the Gods above are my witnesses. King Harishchandra has vowed to give me what I ask for," he said aloud.

"Well then Harishchandra, I ask for your entire kingdom which comprises the whole earth," the sage declared loudly.

"It is yours, my Lord," said Harishchandra without batting an eyelid.

"Very well, I accept your gift. But being a king you

ought to know that every gift to a Brahmin should be followed by a *dakshina* (cash gift). Where is my *dakshina,* Harishchandra?"

"I am sorry, I had forgotten. I shall ask my treasurer to give you a hundred gold coins immediately," said Harishchandra.

"Your treasurer?" Vishwamitra laughed. "Nothing is yours any more! Have you forgotten that you have just gifted me the entire earth with whatever it contains? The gold coins are not yours to give away. In fact, the very land you are standing on now belongs to me and you have no right to stay here."

Harishchandra hung his head. He realised that he now owned nothing on earth.

"Better pay me my *dakshina* and then go out of my land with your wife and son," said Vishwamitra.

The people in Harishchandra's kingdom were shocked at the happenings. They felt sad for themselves and their pious king too. They begged Vishwamitra to have mercy and return Harishchandra a small fraction of his kingdom.

"No, I shall not," said Vishwamitra sternly. "Not even as much as the ground under his feet. Harishchandra has made a gift of his kingdom. It will be a shame asking for it back."

"I am not asking anything back, my Lord," pleaded Harishchandra, "But if I may not live in a corner of your land, amidst my people where should I live?"

"Varanasi is not part of your kingdom," said Vishwamitra. "It is the abode of Shiva. You may go and live there with your wife and son, but not until you have paid me my *dakshina*. I don't care how you raise it, but you must give it to me."

Harishchandra promised to give it at any cost before sunset. He then went to his wife Queen Taramati. She had already heard everything. But she was a brave woman and was determined to stand by her husband. "We have no time to lose, my Lord," she told her husband.

"What matters more than anything else is your promise to Vishwamitra. Since we have nothing to call our own, you must sell me and raise the money," the queen said, "Ask the people if anyone is willing to buy a maid and pay the money to the old sage."

"I cannot do any such thing, Taramati," said Harishchandra breaking down, "You are the queen of this land, not just my wife. As your husband I am bound to protect you all my life. How could I possibly sell you and that too, to a commoner?"

"I am no longer a queen, just as you are no longer a king," said Taramati, "Keeping your word is more important than protecting me. Come, my Lord. It's getting late. The sun will set before long."

Harishchandra dried his eyes and walked to the market place with Taramati and Rohit.

His voice did not shake as he cried, "Does anyone need a maid? Please speak up if you do. You can have her for four thousand gold pieces."

An old Brahmin, who needed someone to do all his housework, came forward and paid the money. As Taramati was about to leave, little Rohit started crying and held firmly to her sari.

"Please let him come with me," pleaded Taramati. "I cannot leave him alone."

"No, I cannot feed two people," said the Brahmin. "Besides, he will be of no use to me, only a bother."

"I shall feed him from my share of food and see that he does not trouble anyone," begged Taramati. The Brahmin finally agreed to take both of them with him.

When Harishchandra paid the money to Vishwamitra, the sage did not seem pleased.

"This is far too little to be considered *dakshina*. I must have at least one hundred more gold coins."

"But I have nothing else to sell, my Lord," said Harishchandra. "My wife and son were all I could call my own and I have sold them both."

"You have yourself, don't you?" said Vishwamitra. "Aren't you worth anything at all?"

"I hadn't thought about it," said Harishchandra. "You shall have your *dakshina*, I promise."

Harishchandra went to the market place once more and offered himself. "Does anyone need a slave? Give me hundred gold coins and you can buy me," he shouted in despair. A man, who used to cremate the dead on the banks of the Ganga, needed a helper. He paid the money to Harishchandra and took him along. Harishchandra gave the money to Vishwamitra and at last was free from his debt.

But life was unthinkably tough for Harishchandra. He worked throughout the day and there was never a moment's respite. And of course there was no question of payment because Harishchandra was now a slave.

Queen Taramati fared no better because she too had to work all day long. She had very little to eat as most of the food she received, she gave to her son Rohit. One day the Brahmin said that he could not have Rohit playing about all day, doing nothing.

"But he is far too young to work," said Taramati.

"He is not too young to pick flowers for my *puja*," said the Brahmin, "Let him go to the woods every morning and fetch them. There shall be no meal for him unless he gets my flowers."

So at the crack of dawn, Rohit would go to the forest and pick up flowers in time for the Brahmin's *puja*. One morning, as he was picking up flowers in the dark, a venomous snake bit him. Rohit screamed and was dead long before anyone could reach him.

Taramati was worried when it got late and there was no trace of Rohit. She rushed to the woods and saw him lying under a *champak* tree.

"My precious, what has happened to you?" cried Taramati as she picked up the child in her arms. His body had turned blue due to the snake poison. When she realised that her son was dead, she cried and cried.

She returned home crying her heart out. *There is nothing left to live for,* Taramati thought sadly.

The Brahmin looked at them and asked Taramati to go to River Ganga and get her dead son cremated.

"But I have no money to buy the wood or anything else needed for the ritual," said Taramati, "My Rohit is a prince, after all."

"A prince! He is the poor son of a maid," said the Brahmin. "Go and request the slaves at the *ghat* to cremate him free. Perhaps one of them will oblige."

Taramati carried Rohit's body in her arms and walked to the banks of the Ganga. She put his body down and burst into tears. "Where are you, Harishchandra? See the plight of your own, dear Rohit! I don't even have the money to cremate him decently! Oh, what have I done to deserve this cruel fate? How am I to live without my child?"

Harishchandra, who had been setting fire to one of the pyres, heard her cry. When he heard the grieved mother call out his own name and that of Rohit, he rushed out. At first he did not recognise Taramati. Nor did she recognise Harishchandra. After all both of them looked haggard and were in tattered clothes. But when Harishchandra looked at Rohit's angelic face, he recognised him instantly and burst into tears.

"Is this indeed my precious Rohit?" he cried, "And are you really Taramati? Tell me what has happened to him. Oh, I can't believe this! Why couldn't I die instead of him?"

"He got bitten by a snake," said Taramati in a broken voice, "I have no money. I know you have none either. Can you chop some wood and cremate our child? We don't have much time."

"Yes, I shall do that for our son," said Harishchandra with a heavy heart.

Just as Harishchandra was about to lift Rohit's body and place it on the pyre, sage Vishwamitra arrived there miraculously. He touched Rohit's forehead and said, "Get up my dear." Rohit sat up rubbing his eyes.

Before the astonished Harishchandra or Taramati could utter a word, Vishwamitra smiled at them and said, "Harishchandra, I hope you forgive me for all the hardship that I put you through. I have been testing your generosity all this time. I wanted to see whether you are really able to give away everything from your heart and without resentment. It is not an easy thing to do. But I am now satisfied that you are the greatest *daata* (giver) on the earth. Return to your kingdom with your wife and son with my blessings. You will live to be one of the greatest kings ever born!"

Harishchandra and Taramati touched Vishwamitra's feet in gratitude. Turning back they saw their own chariot waiting for them to take them back to Ayodhya.

When Revati Fell From Heaven....

Long, long ago there lived a sage named Ritavak. He was childless for a long time. When he was blessed with a son finally, Ritavak was overjoyed. But his happiness was short-lived. Despite all his teachings, his son grew to be a good-for-nothing fellow – lazy, unprincipled and wicked. Unfortunately, after his birth, his family suffered several misfortunes. His wife caught an incurable and painful disease, and the sage suffered from a variety of ailments.

Sage Ritavak was unhappy and puzzled. He went to sage Garg for advice.

"What do you think could be the reason for all these things happening to me? I can't think of any wrong that I have committed, to deserve such unhappiness."

Sage Garg closed his eyes and meditated silently for a while.

"Your suffering is not due to any of your actions, Ritavak. It is because your son was born under an unlucky star, Revati."

"But that was not my fault! What can I do to save the situation?" cried Ritavak.

"It's very unfortunate is all I can say," said Garg.

"A mere star has no right to ruin my life," said Ritavak, "especially when I have done nothing to deserve it."

Ritavak was seething with rage. He cursed Revati, the unlucky star, to fall down from the sky. Ritavak was a great sage so his curse carried tremendous power. Revati fell from the sky and landed on top of the Kumud mountain. Its light lit up the entire mountainside and all the forests, caves, rocks and waterfalls around it. Part of the light rolled down to the valley below and turned into a crystal clear lake. A beautiful girl was born from the water of the crystal lake.

Sage Pramucha, who had his hermitage in the Kumud valley, discovered the baby girl. Surprised to see so much light all of a sudden, he went to the mountainside to see what had happened. When he saw the baby lying on the bank of the newly created lake, he took her home. The sage brought up the child like his own daughter and named her 'Revati' after the fallen star.

Revati grew up to be a radiantly beautiful girl. Pramucha loved her dearly and was worried where he would find her a worthy husband. He could think of no one who seemed good enough for her.

Finally, he put the question to Agni, the fire God.

"Do not worry about Revati, Pramucha," said Agni. "The great King Durgam, who is perfect in every way, will come to your hermitage some day and will marry her. Wait patiently for the day and all will be well."

Pramucha was very happy and returned home.

A few days later King Durgam was out on a hunting trip. He was passing that way and decided to drop in at sage Pramucha's hermitage, just as Agni had predicted. Revati was picking flowers in the garden when he arrived. "Is sage Pramucha in?" Durgam asked Revati. "I would like to pay him my respects."

"Please wait, and I shall tell father that you are here," said Revati.

"Are you sage Pramucha's daughter?" asked Durgam, struck by her radiant beauty.

"Yes, I am," replied Revati and she went inside the cottage.

Pramucha had heard them talking and came out at once. His joy knew no bounds when he discovered that it was none other than King Durgam himself. He called Gautam, his chief disciple and said, "Gautam, arrange for a special welcome ritual. King Durgam is not just my guest today; he is also my future son-in-law. So I must welcome him properly."

King Durgam was astonished at Pramucha's words. He touched the sage's feet and said, "My Lord, what did you mean by saying that I am your future son-in-law? I know nothing about it and have no marriage plans."

"My dear, I should have explained before," said sage Pramucha smiling at him. "You have seen my daughter Revati, haven't you?"

"Yes I have, but..."

"It is destined that you should wed her. Agni, the fire God has said so, and I know she is worthy of being your queen. She is as good as she is beautiful. You have no objections, do you?"

"No, my Lord. I would be honoured if Revati marries me. She is the most beautiful girl I have ever seen," replied King Durgam.

The inmates of the hermitage rejoiced at the news, for Revati was very dear to them all. They got busy preparing for the wedding.

Sage Pramucha called Revati aside and asked, "I hope you are happy with my choice, Revati? Actually, it was God Agni who had told me that King Durgam would marry you. I think you are a very lucky girl!"

"I have nothing to say about your choice, father, but there is a special request that I should like to make. I hope you will grant me my wish."

"Of course," said Pramucha unhesitatingly. "What is it, my daughter?"

"I would like to be married under the Revati star," said Revati.

"Good heavens, what a strange thing to ask for!" exclaimed sage Pramucha, "But it is not possible, my dear. Revati is no longer a star and is no longer in the sky."

"Why not?" asked Revati amazed.

"It fell down from heaven because of sage Ritavak's

curse. It came crashing down on Kumud mountain which has been called Raivatak ever since."

"But, father, I had taken a solemn vow to wed only under the Revati star," said Revati obstinately, "I cannot marry otherwise."

Sage Pramucha looked worried. "My child, you have placed me in a strange problem. I have already promised King Durgam to wed you to him. How can I face him or anyone else if I do not keep my word?"

"But father, you promised to grant me my wish too," said Revati.

"Why are you so insistent about the Revati Star? There are plenty of others, far better in every way. I shall choose a really good star for your wedding."

"I don't want any other star. I want the Revati," said Revati in a determined voice.

"I really don't know what to do," said sage Pramucha losing his patience. "I never imagined you could be so disobedient!"

"But why should it be such a problem, father?" asked Revati. "If sage Ritavak could knock it off the sky, could you not put it back once again? I don't think you are less powerful than sage Ritavak."

A sudden smile lit up sage Pramucha's face. "You are quite right, Revati. I didn't think of that. Of course, I can put the star back where she belongs."

Pramucha sat down to pray and the power of his *tapasya* was strong enough to put Revati back amidst the other stars.

Revati, the daughter of Pramucha, and King Durgam were married and they left for their new abode.

Revati, the star, became a part of the original constellation, shining bright once again!